CW00853085

CATHETER BOY

Written by
Alfie Exelby

Illustrated by
Nancy Exelby

Please scan this QR code to follow Alfie and Nancy Exelby's journey to making this book a reality. You can also watch a celebrity read the book on CBeebies!

MAPLE
PUBLISHERS

Catheter Boy

Author: Alfie Exelby

Copyright © Alfie Exelby (2023)

The right of Alfie Exelby to be identified as author of this work has been asserted by the authors in accordance with section 77 and 78 of the Copyright, Designs and Patents Act 1988.

First Published in 2023

ISBN 978-1-915796-18-9 (Paperback)

Cover Illustration by: Sarah Exelby

Book layout by:
  Maple Publishers
  www.maplepublishers.com

Published by:
  Maple Publishers
  Fairbourne Drive, Atterbury,
  Milton Keynes,
  MK10 9RG, UK
  www.maplepublishers.com

A CIP catalogue record for this title is available from the British Library.

*By Alfie Exelby, age 8 (this actually happened!!!),
except I didn't turn into a superhero of course!
Illustrations by Nancy Exelby, age 9
(but the cover illustration is by Mummy,
Sarah Exelby)*

Sarah, Nancy and Alfie would like to give special thanks to a few people who have brought this book to life.

Angela Arnison's kind donation has turned publishing the story from a dream to a reality. Everyone who has donated to support the children's hospital and catheter boy journey. The Sheffield Children's Hospital for all of Alfie's care.

Last but not the least Nanny Janny whose endless love and support has got us here.

A word from the author...

When I was born, one of my kidneys failed so the Doctor took it out. I've always had to go to the hospital to have my blood taken and have scans to check the kidney I have left is working properly.

When we were locked down because of Covid, I didn't have any tests. When I did, my kidney had gone from working at 60% down to 40%! This was not good. They told my Mum and me that I would have a suprapubic catheter put into my bladder. This means a tube would come out of my tummy and the wee goes into a bag attached to my leg.

My Mum explained to me that lots of people have catheters and you don't know by just looking at them. She said maybe some Superheroes might have one, and she said "What powers do you think they would have?"

This got me thinking, so I wrote a little book about a boy who turns into 'Catheter Boy' after his operation. Luckily, my sister Nancy is really good at art so she's the illustrator!

(Apart from the front cover, my mummy drew this when she explained to me that I needed a Cathetar.) When I went to the hospital, my Mum told the doctor about my story. She said that she would really like to give my book to other boys and girls who have to have catheters to cheer them up and to make the whole process a little bit less scary.

Jon Richardson has heard about my book and has read it for CBeeBies! Please scan the QR code to watch it, it's hillarious!

I have been raising money for the Children's Hospital because they look after me. I also want my story to be available worldwide so other kids can read it and hopefully not feel as scared about the Catheter.

Thank you so much.

Alfie Exelby (8)

It starts in an ordinary house and ordinary people live in it. The people in this house are: Mum - Sarah, me - Alfie, my sister - Nancy, and our cute, small, black malti-poo, Lola (dog). We are the crazy Exelby family. Today I sit on the sofa watching television and all of a sudden my mum comes in and says "you're going for your catheter operation tomorrow!" and I think in my head how exciting it's going to be.

At 7:15 we leave the house, drop Nancy off with our Nanny Janny, and then go to The Sheffield Children's Hospital. First thing to do is to get into the surgery room by asking the receptionist where it is. In the surgery room I beat my Mum playing the card game Uno four times in a row! She gets two wins because we play six rounds.

Illustrated by Alfie Exelby

At 11:11 I go for surgery. I feel nervous so the doctors let my Mum ride on the bed with me! My Mum and me go zooming in the wheely bed down to theatre and they give me a breathing mask that makes me go to sleep.

When I wake up, I'm going to be… CATHETER BOY!!!! It turns out that the Suprapubic Catheter doesn't just help save my only kidney but also has given me superpowers!!

Day 1 as Catheter Boy. There's no time to rest up, I think that I need to design my suit in my head for a moment... Eureka! So, my suit is going to be yellow of course, boots: red, cape: orange. I look in my wardrobe for clothes in the colours I've chosen, find my Nannan Brenda's sewing machine and get to work. I try it on, ooh it looks nice!

My phone rings, I can't believe it! The Avengers have heard about my new powers and are calling me for a mission in Italy - a lava monster to defeat. Ok, let's do this. I pack my suitcase (making sure I don't forget my Catheter Boy Suit) and fly to Italy using my magic cape.

All of a sudden the ground begins to shake. "There's a volcano" I shout loudly to the people around "RUN!!!" I fly into the air and suddenly "there is a L-L-Lava Monster!!!" The battle starts. The lava monster sprays lava at my leg, it hurts so much my heart rate drops. I check to see if he hit my bag, luckily not. The Lava Monster hits me with his lava hot fist and I manage to dodge it. Show time - I wee on the Lava Monster by opening my [catheter] Flip Flow all over him! The Lava Monster is defeated!

The Lava Monster...Grrrrrr

After my victory over the Lava Monster, I fly to America to eat some burger and fries in The Big Apple. Suddenly, I notice some plants - one starts moving. There is a Venus Human-Trap!! The Venus Human-Trap eats people alive... "RUN!!!" I shout. Everyone around me knocks everything off the table and runs. Everyone apart from little Jimmy sat at the table, who throws his burger at the Venus Human-Trap. The Venus Human-Trap eats the burger, eats little Jimmy, then BURPS LOUDLY.

Right, that's it, the battle is on! The Venus Human-Trap jumps towards me and bites me on the leg, piercing my bag fiercely. The wee sprays into it's mouth and kills it "ha ha I killed you!!!"

When I leave the diner, crowds of people are chanting "Catheter Boy! Catheter Boy!" I feel good, apart from thinking about little Jimmy of course.

Then I turn around, little Jimmy is stood behind me. He was burped out...phew!

I finish my tasty burger and fly to Australia. Suddenly there's a tsunami and jellyfish start to raid the land and the leader is… Jerry the Jellyfish!

The jellyfish sting everyone on the land and I quickly remember that urine helps with jellyfish stings. So I fly into the air, open my catheter bag and wee on everybody to stop the sting. The battle begins with Jerry and he stings me on my foot, OUCH! I open the bag and spray it on myself to stop the sting then I wee on Jerry with the Flip Flow. Jerry dies!

N ext up is to save the environment by watering all the plants in the world (by watering all the plants, I mean I'm going to wee on them).

Ok, first I'm going to fly to Scotland and wee everywhere on the plants. I accidentally wee on a Scottish lady, her boyfriend shouts at me for doing it.... "oops, sorry!" Ok, now that I've saved Scotland I'm going to wee on England. I fly to England and wee on all the plants in England. After that I visit Wales to open the bag and let the wee out, spray it everywhere and water the plants to save the environment. Next stop Italy. Ok, since I'm at Italy it's time to have a nice, tasty pizza of course! Right, now that I've eaten a nice, tasty pizza I'm going to wee everywhere else. Ok, now that I've done Italy, I'm going to do... Ukraine, WOW - there are lots and lots of sunflowers! I carry on fertilising the plants all around the world.

My job for now is done. Time to return to The Sheffield Children's Hospital to have my [catheter] MIC-KEY button fitted and check my kidney function.

The Children's Hospital Charity Bear – Theo

Illustrated by Nancy Exelby

THE END

Milton Keynes UK
Ingram Content Group UK Ltd.
UKHW022023221023
431136UK00008B/22